The Real Story

Sergio Ruzzier

Abrams Appleseed
New York

What?!

MOUSE!

Yes, Cat?

What is this?

It looks like a broken
cookie jar to me.

I know it is a
broken cookie jar!

How did it happen?
And where are the cookies?

Those are good questions.
Let me explain . . .

The cookies were tired of being closed inside.
So they started jumping up and down
and side to side until the jar fell and broke.

Finally free, they are now running around the countryside having a good time.

Honestly, we should be happy for them.

Mouse, that's not possible.
Cookies can't run.
Tell me the real story.

Okay. Let's see . . .

A slimy monster knocked at our door. He wanted to know if he could have a cookie. I said, "Sure, serve yourself." So he grabbed the jar, but it slipped out of his slimy hands, fell, and broke.

At that point I told him he could have all the cookies.

He picked them up, said "Thank you," and left.

Slimy monsters don't exist, Mouse.
Tell me the real story.

Well then,
how about . . .

An alien named Georgette came by and said
her cookie-fueled spaceship was out of cookies.

So I gave her some, but in the excitement she
knocked the jar over, which fell and broke.

She was very sorry about it, but I told her,
"No worries, and have a good trip."

Georgette is not a likely
name for an alien, Mouse.
Tell me the real story!

Fine. Here it is.

A bug came in and asked if she could have just one cookie. So I gave her one. Then she asked if I could give cookies to her cousins, too.

I said yes, but I couldn't have guessed
how many cousins that little bug had.

Oh, and then the jar fell and broke.

Mouse, I don't believe your stories.

TELL ME THE REAL STORY NOW!

Oh, you want the real story?
I understand.
I will tell you the real story, then.

I stole and ate all the
cookies, and then
the jar fell and broke.

The end.

That's such a boring story.

I know it is.

Can you tell me another cookie story?

Sure. May I have a cookie first?

To Isla and Ruby

The illustrations for this book were made
with pen and ink and watercolor.

Cataloging-in-Publication Data has been applied for
and may be obtained from the Library of Congress.

ISBN 978-1-4197-5526-2

Book design by Natalie Padberg Bartoo

Printed and bound in China
10 9 8 7 6 5 4 3 2 1

For bulk discount inquiries, contact specialsales@abramsbooks.com.

ABRAMS The Art of Books
195 Broadway, New York, NY 10007
abramsbooks.com